Let's Read About Food

Bread and Cereal

by Cynthia Klingel and Robert B. Noyed
photographs by Gregg Andersen

Reading consultant: Cecilia Minden-Cupp, Ph.D.,
Adjunct Professor, College of Continuing and Professional Studies, University of Virginia

For a free color catalog describing
Weekly Reader® Early Learning Library's
list of high-quality books, call 1-800-542-2595
or fax your request to (414) 332-3567.

Library of Congress Cataloging-in-Publication Data available
upon request from publisher. Fax (414) 336-0157 for the
attention of the Publishing Records Department.

ISBN 0-8368-3055-5 (lib. bdg.)
ISBN 0-8368-3144-6 (softcover)

This edition first published in 2002 by
Weekly Reader® Early Learning Library
330 West Olive Street, Suite 100
Milwaukee, WI 53212 USA

An Editorial Directions book
Editors: E. Russell Primm and Emily Dolbear
Art direction, design, and page production: The Design Lab
Photographer: Gregg Andersen
Weekly Reader® Early Learning Library art direction: Tammy Gruenewald
Weekly Reader® Early Learning Library production: Susan Ashley

Printed in the United States of America

1 2 3 4 5 6 7 8 9 06 05 04 03 02

Note to Educators and Parents

As a Reading Specialist I know that books for young children should engage their interest, impart useful information, and motivate them to want to learn more.

Let's Read About Food is a new series of books designed to help children understand the value of good nutrition and eating to stay healthy.

A young child's active mind is engaged by the carefully chosen subjects. The imaginative text works to build young vocabularies. The short, repetitive sentences help children stay focused as they develop their own relationship with reading. The bright, colorful photographs of children enjoying good nutrition habits complement the text with their simplicity and both entertain and encourage young children to want to learn – and read – more.

These books are designed to be used by adults as "read-to" books to share with children to encourage early literacy in the home, school, and library. They are also suitable for more advanced young readers to enjoy on their own.

– Cecilia Minden-Cupp, Ph.D.,
Adjunct Professor, College of Continuing and Professional Studies, University of Virginia

I like to eat bread and cereal. They are good for me.

We choose from six different kinds of food. We need to eat all six kinds every day to stay healthy.

fats and sweets
SODA POP
milk and cheese
YOGURT
meat
PEANUT BUTTER
vegetables
fruit
FRUIT JUICE
bread and cereal

My body gets energy and vitamins from bread and cereal. These foods help me run and play.

Sometimes I
have cold cereal
for breakfast.
Sometimes I
have hot cereal.

Pasta and rice are cereals. Pasta and rice come in different colors!

Pasta comes in many shapes. Sometimes it is hard to keep on my fork!

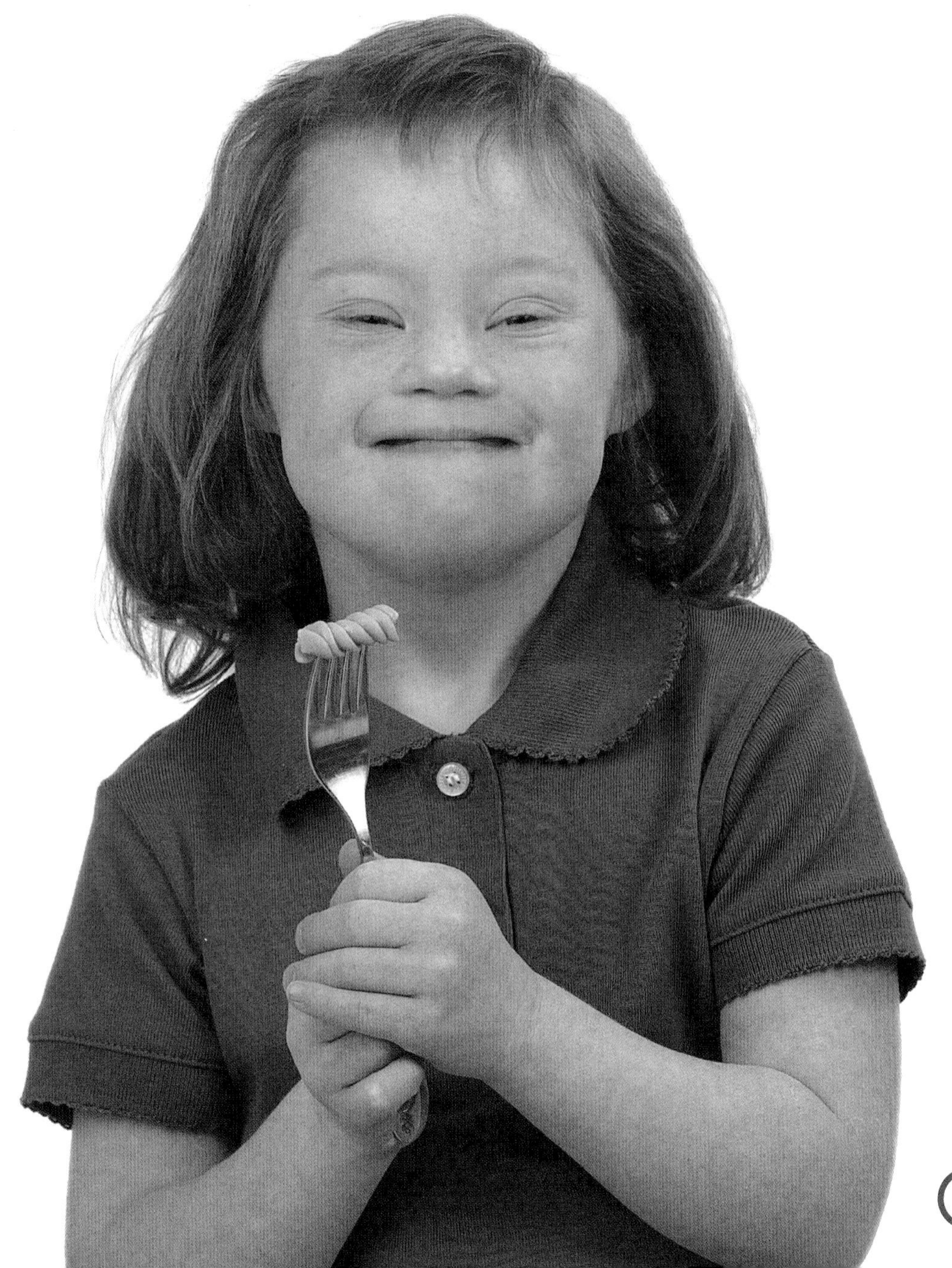

Mom says popcorn, pretzels, and crackers are good snacks.

Bread comes in different shapes. Tortillas and bagels are round. French bread is long and skinny.

I am hungry for
a big bowl of
pretzels!

Glossary

bagel–round, chewy roll with a hole in the middle

pretzel–dough that is shaped into a stick or knot shape and baked

tortilla–round, flat bread made from cornmeal or flour

vitamin–one of the substances in food that is needed for good health

For More Information

Fiction Books

Davis, Matt. *The Baizel Berry Bread.* Los Angeles: Cobblestone, 1997.

Krensky, Stephen, and Marc Tolon Brown. *Arthur and the Crunch Cereal Contest.* Boston: Little, Brown, 1998.

Nonfiction Books

Morris, Ann, and Ken Heyman. *Bread Bread.* New York: Mulberry Books, 1993.

Web Sites

Bread Basics

www.breadbasics.com/

For more fun facts about bread

Bread—Science Museum of Minnesota

www.smm.org/sln/tf/b/bread/bread.html

For more about bread and how to grow your own bread mold

Index

About the Authors

Cynthia Klingel has worked as a high school English teacher and an elementary school teacher. She is currently the curriculum director for a Minnesota school district. Cynthia Klingel lives with her family in Mankato, Minnesota.

Robert B. Noyed started his career as a newspaper reporter. Since then, he has worked in school communications and public relations at the state and national level. Robert B. Noyed lives with his family in Brooklyn Center, Minnesota.